Christmas Stories
from
Celrin Fairies

PAMELA MAY JONES

ISBN 978-1-956010-88-6 (paperback)
ISBN 978-1-956010-89-3 (digital)

Rushmore Press LLC
1 800 460 9188
www.rushmorepress.com

Printed in the United States of America

THE ANGEL WHO FORGOT CHRISTMAS

By Pamela May Jones copyright 2012

It was a very, very cold day in November when Carole the Christmas Angel was about her duties trying to organise the Christmas Elves and Fairies into getting their jobs done in time to prepare for Christmas Day.

Christmas Day was one of the busiest times for Angels, Fairies and Elves. They were the ones who helped Santa and Mamma Claus making, painting, wrapping and delivering the presents with Santa. He could not do all he did on his own he had a very good team in the Christmas Brigade as he called them. The Christmas Brigade and the Reindeers, that is what made Christmas for Santa and Mamma Claus.

Along with Jack Frost the Christmas Fairy and the Winter Fairy they are what made Christmas fun. Plenty of food, plenty to drink, Mamma made a nice punch out of all the different berries she collected through the year and kept in her new freezer with the help of Jack Frost. He worked throughout the year to help Mamma keep everything frozen until Christmas week. Normally, he slept most of the year or until another job came from abroad somewhere where they needed frost and snow. His cousin the Winter Fairy usually went with him on these trips to help other countries, which needed snow and ice to help them make money by providing the holidaymakers with ice and snow. People, who loved to ski and skate, use a toboggan or snowboard.

Then there were the logs to cut and stack ready for Santa and Mamma to sit in front of, when Christmas Eve was done, and they could relax. They had a daughter called Carole she was the invisible daughter of Santa and Mamma, only they could see her as she was the Christmas Fairy and no one was supposed to see her. The only time they could see her was when she appeared in the night sky on Christmas Eve, just like she did the night Jesus was born.

Santa, Mamma and Carole were very old in years but they never looked it because they were special people. They had what was called Christmas Magic. Only very special people had it, as it was very, very rare indeed. They used a special thing called fairy dust, each of the colours of fairy dust was used for different things. Rainbow fairy dust was used to protect the people of Celrin. Santa used it to keep the dome bright and clear so that nothing evil could get into Celrin and cause harm. Like nasty Goblins, gremlins, warlocks and very bad wizards. Only good wizards could live in Celrin like William and Walter, they were father and son, everyone teased William they nick named him little Willie Wizard because his grandfather had been called William and it got confusing when they were all together.

Then you had purple fairy dust, which you could use to time travel like Pippa Plum, Mr. Wumba the pygmy, Rollie Pollie the Clown Penguin and his friends and also Mr. Theodore Smith. Mr. Wumba, Rolllie Pollie and friends and Mr. Wumba all used a big black cooking pot to time travel in. Mr. Theodore Smith was special like Pippa Plum they only had to draw a circle and put in the purple fairy dust for it to work. Then the wind would come and twirled around them until it became a tornado whisking them up into the centre and as they said the magic words it would set them down wherever they wanted to go.

Mr Theodore Smith was a time traveller, who was a friend of Red Beard the pirate. They would get their booty from Spanish Galleons, like the one they sailed in. Which Rollie Pollie found in the Antarctic when he discovered that part of the ice which should have been frozen was not, and he dived in to see why and as he dove, down, down, down he found the Spanish Galleon. Then his friend Esmeralda had discovered the Captains log and the big, black cooking pot with the purple fairy dust. They then time travelled to Burmuda to find the pirates treasure. They have lots more adventures going to see Lolly Molly and visit all her friends in Celrin.

Now Pippa Plum was a time travelling archaeologist she went around the world trying to find and give back all the treasures that had been stolen from various places, like the Jade Healing Mask of the Glummpopo. She time travelled to the Glummpopo Village and found them inside a dome similar to the one Celrin had. They were supposed to be a lost tribe but it just turned out that they were inside the dome and could not be seen outside it. They had marvellous treasures in this village various masks for different things like healing, seeing into the future. Masses of gold items. jewels beyond compare, silver, and different metals no one knew about. They had meteorites, which had fallen from the sky and they had worked their magical skills making things with it which were absolutely beautiful it was almost as if no one had created them their skills were so good.

Now, lets get back to our story of the Angel who forgot Christmas.
It was the eve before Christmas Eve and everyone was almost ready with the things they had to do. There were just a few things to finish painting. Some things had to be screwed together and then they would be ready. The Christmas Angel was flying up into the top of the building to make sure that the roof would open correctly on the night Santa would be out delivering his christmas toys. When all of a sudden the beam slipped some how and it hit the Christmas Angel on the head knocking her to the ground.
'Angel, Angel called the little fairies and elves are you alright?'
Angel looked at them in disbelief, 'who are you she said?'
'Angel it's your friends from Santa's House and Toy Factory.'
'Santa whose Santa?' asked Angel.

'Oh! Dear said the little fairies she's lost her memory.'

'What are we going to do said the little elves?' 'We need her to remember what to do this night is so special.'

'Lets take her to Mamma and Santa and they might be able to help her.'

'Mamma, mamma cried the little fairy folk it's the Christmas Angel the beam fell down on her and it hit her head and now she cannot remember us or anything'

'What are we going to do Mamma said to Santa?'

'Without the Christmas Angel we cannot have Christmas.'

'No one can take her place in the sky and without her the New Year cannot begin.'

'We must make her comfortable and see how things go' said Santa.

'Mamma put a cold compress on her head and let her sleep for a while.'

'Now go away and do your jobs little ones said Santa you cannot help her.'

'Yes Santa' they called, not looking very happy and away they went to finish their jobs.

'What will happen if the Christmas Fairy cannot fly into the sky, how can we make Christmas?'

'Do not know said the chief elf we must just pray.'

'Please dear lord said the Chief Elf please make the Christmas Angel better so she can make Christmas.'

'They all said Amen.' and carried on finishing their tasks.

'How are you now Angel asked Mamma Claus?'

'Feel funny said Angel.' I feel I have forgotten something I must do.'

'Well should I tell you said Mamma Claus?'

'Yes, please said Angel if you can help me.'

'Well, said Mamma Claus you are a special Angel you fly up into the night sky on Christmas Eve and you turn into a star the one who guided the three wise men to Jesus, Mary and Joseph.'

'Goodness, said Angel how could I forget that?'

'But how do I change into a star?' she asked.

'Well, no one else knows' said Mamma Claus.

'Well, I cannot remember either' she said.

'My head hurts so much.' She said.

'Never mind that now dear, take these two little pills Santa made for you and have a little sleep. We still have twelve hour before we need to worry.'

'Thank you,' she said and took the little pills.

She was soon fast asleep and Mamma Claus crept softly away. She was talking to Santa about Angel, 'I am very worried' she said.

'She cannot remember how to turn into a star.' Said Mamma.

'I cannot help her.' Said Santa. 'I do not know how she does it.'

'Well, perhaps if one or two of the other Angels take her up into the night sky she may be able to remember once she gets up there.' Said Santa.

'Well, I suppose we can give it a try.' Said Mamma almost in tears. 'Now, now dearest' said Santa 'do not take on so.'

'God will help in our time of need.' Said Santa.

'Now make us some of your lovely fairy tea, you know the one, raspberry, strawberry and blueberry.' Said Santa 'it will calm our nerves.'

So Mamma Claus flew into the kitchen almost on tiptoe doing what Santa asked. She made the tea and added some mince pies to the tray with some of her fairy cream to top them. 'Here we are Santa called Mamma.' As she set the tray down before him. 'Oh! Mamma you are a dear, how did you know I was thinking of mince pies.'

'Well, I did not really she said but its Christmas Eve nearly, so I brought you some.'

'Well, said Santa they are wonderful as usual the fairy dust makes all the difference.' 'Well, it helps me a great deal said Mamma because when I sprinkle it on the top of my cakes before they go into the oven, they always fly out perfect to go on the cooling tray she laughed.' 'It is because I do not have to watch them all the time.'

'I can get on with other things.' Like ironing your shirts.' she said laughing her tinkling laugh.

'Mm. She said just the job.'

'Now I must check on Angel' she said. She peeped in at Angel she was still fast asleep. 'Good' she said to herself, sleep is the best thing for getting better.

'How is she asked Santa?'

'She is still asleep' said Mamma Claus.

'Good' said Santa with a sigh. 'Just what she needs.'

'Suddenly, they heard crying, someone sobbing their little heart out.'

'Good gracious' said Santa. 'Is that Angel?'

'I am afraid so, said Mamma as she flew into the other room to check on Angel.

'Whatever is the matter dear?' she said.

'I cannot remember Christmas or how to become a Christmas Star.' She said crying into Mamma's two cradling arms. 'There, there now my pet' she said.

'Santa and I have come up with a plan.' 'We thought that if we sent you up into the night sky with two or three of your friends. Once you're up there, you may remember.'

'That sounds alright, if it works but what if it does not work?' said Angel.

'Well, we will have to wait and see.' Said Santa 'now here's Mamma with one of her nice mince pies and cream and some fairy tea.' 'Here you are said Mamma, now sit and enjoy these.

'Thank you said Angel.' 'You're so kind to me.'

'Well, you have always been kind to us dear' said Mamma.

'We will leave you now, we still have a few hours work to do,' said Santa.

'Can I help you?' said Angel.

'No dear you just sit and rest.'

'Santa, Santa called the little elves, we have another problem.'

'Now what said Santa?'

It's Rudolf he cannot get his nose to glow since he's had that cold.'

'Goodness, first no star to guide us now no red nose either.'

'I am cursed this year.' said Santa laughing. He always-laughed even in times of trouble he was happy. It must be his cheery countenance.

'He was whistling as he thought what to do?'

'Oh! Mamma I'm so stupid he said.

'Why dear?' asked Mamma.

'It's been staring me in the face, all day fairy dust, the special fairy dust we keep for emergencies he said. The special rainbow fairy dust that all the fairy folk put in the special pot to protect us all, maybe that will help Angel as well as Rudolf.'

'Good Gracious me.' Of course said Mamma. 'Shall I bring it down from its special place?'

'Yes, dear we are running out of time, we must try anything and everything.'

Mamma flew upstairs and into the special cabinet to fetch the special pot of fairy dust. Then she flew back down again with it to give it to Santa. 'Here dear' she said handing him the little pot, which grew bigger and bigger as soon as he put it onto the ground. 'Eric, Eric, called Santa.

'Take this to Rudolph please and add it to his hay.'

'Yes, Santa' Eric the Elf said.

Eric ran with it to Rudolph's Stable and did as Santa bid him, added it to the hay and gave it to Rudolph, saying here we are Rudolph this should help you, Santa just thought of it.' Rudolph munched and munched and sure enough the Minute he ate all the hay his nose started to glow. 'I can smell the hay' shouted Rudolph. 'Of course you can you're better because of the special fairy dust. Said Eric laughing at Rudolph as he patted him on the back. 'Now I must go and speak to Santa to tell him the good news.' Said Eric.

'Santa said 'wonderful.' 'Now let's hope it will help Angel.'

'Mamma took some of the fairy dust into Angel in some fairy tea, drink this dear it might help.'

'Angel drank the tea with the special fairy dust in it and asked, 'what is it supposed to do?'

'Help you remember Christmas' said Mamma laughing.

'Angel drank the tea, but nothing is happening,' she cried.

'Sit still a while and wait' said Santa smiling, it might take some time.'

A couple of hours went by, nothing yet,' said Mamma looking very worried. 'We only have thirty minutes left before we need to set off' said Santa.

'I will help her change into her new dress of gold' said Mamma.

They went upstairs and Angel and Mamma sorted Angels hair and put on her new dress and brushed her white feathered wings tinted with gold. 'Anything yet, dear' asked Mamma. ' No, said Angel almost crying.' 'Now, now dear said Mamma, don't start to cry or you will mess up your nice new dress.'

'I will go and get Seraphina and Angelina, they can go with you.' Said Mamma.

'Time to go Angel' said Santa.

'I'm ready, but I still cannot remember how to change into the Christmas Star.'

'Maybe it will come when you're up there.' Said Santa.

'I do hope so,' said Angel.

'Ready girls' called Santa calling to the three Angels.

'Yes.' Santa we are ready.

'Onward my reindeer friends' called Santa, Rudolph light up your nose please.' 'Fly upwards my friends he called naming each one in turn.' 'Upwards, forever upwards.'

Soon they were at the point where the Christmas Star would appear, 'here we are my Angels' said Santa. The three Angels flew up into the night sky together. Still Angel did not turn into the Christmas Star. Seraphina and Angelina and Angel held hands, praying unto God to help them.

Still, nothing, poor Santa looked back trying to see if the Christmas Star had appeared. 'Oh! No' poor little Angel thought Santa.

He headed towards Sweden, nothing. Onto Norway and then Denmark, still no Christmas Star. As he turned to go back towards his next village, he could see Seraphina and Angelina. They were glowing in the night sky, all silver and blue. Angel began to cry, when all of a sudden as her tears hit her dress it began to glow golden in the night sky, the more tears Angel cried the more her dress glowed. She could not stop crying but they were tears of happiness because as each tear landed on her dress she was changing into the Christmas Star. God had answered her prayers. All three angels gave thanks unto God for their Christmas Miracle.

THE LITTLE DONKEY
WHO GOT HIS CHRISTMAS WISH

by Pamela Jones copyright 13.10.2013

IT WAS A COLD crisp November day in the most northern part of
Celrin. There were mountains and a valley with lots of good green
grass, alongside a river stood a little barn of red wood with a little
thatched roof. In that little barn there lived a beautiful little donkey
called Jingles, his mother Saffron and his father called Caesar. They
were cared for by a little Gnome whose name was Timothy. Timothy
lived in a little wooden house, painted red with a thatched roof just like
the donkeys barn. He had little yellow window shutters with little cut
out shapes of donkeys; they kept the bad weather out when the snows
came around Christmas time. He had a little red porch with another
yellow door with a cut out donkey but that had a sliding panel so he
could see who was there without opening the door in bad weather.
It had a glass lantern hung outside so in the bad weather he lit it for
anyone who was lost in the snow. It was a magic lantern you could see
it for miles in any direction, it seemed to glow all around the house
so you could see it. Even anyone who was flying by could see it from
above, you see Santa gave this lantern to Timothy it was like the ones
he used. The little Gnome used to work for Santa when he was younger
but now he had been given the task of looking after the donkeys the
father was the one who was at the side of the crib at the birth of Jesus.

So he was given special powers. Only at Christmas were these powers available to him, or in times of trouble.

One day the baby donkey that was called Jingles was out running about the fields beside the river when he espied a little man. 'Hello' little man what are you doing here? Jingles asked. Well, said the little man I have come in search of my brother Timothy. I am Thomas his younger brother and have not seen him for many years.' Oh! The little donkey said he lives just over there he said pointing with his head and neighing in delight at the thought of Timothy having a brother. 'Should I show you? He asked.

'No, but I have brought a message, it's from our mother and father. Who live in Lapland, said the little gnome', to Jingles the little donkey.

'Well, will you come and play with me later the little donkey asked, its lonely here he said all on my own.' The little gnome laughed and said 'I am a bit old for playing' but I will come and talk to you if I may' he said 'before I go back home.' 'Thank you' said the little donkey I would like that.' 'I am having a little brother or sister at Christmas so after that I will have someone to play with.' He said neighing in delight. The little gnome laughed to himself at the delight of the little donkey as he walked towards the lovely red and yellow thatched cottage of his brother Timothy. He knocked on the little knocker of brass a little donkey of course, tap, ta ta, tap, tap, tap, tap went the little donkey. 'Oh! Good gracious me,' Thomas the little gnome laughed at the site of his little brother Thomas. 'What on earth brings you so far from home?' 'Brother it is so good to see you again after all these years.' Thomas said. 'I have a message from mother and father.' 'Are they in good health? Timothy asked. 'Yes, fine but they wanted to know if you could come and stay for Christmas, Santa is throwing a special party.' Thomas said. 'Oh! Dear Timothy said I have the birth of a new baby donkey due then.' I do not think I will be able to come. Unless, I can find someone who could be here, but its Christmas and so it might be impossible.' Timothy said. 'Could you not bring them to Lapland before then? Thomas asked. 'I would need a special fairy dust for that and only Santa and the Little Unicorn of Um' have that' Timothy said. 'Would you like me to return to Lapland and get some? Thomas asked. 'That would be good, if you could get some of Santa's special fairy dust we could come then.' Timothy said. 'It would be good to go and see mother and father and of course Santa and Mamma Christmas. Will Carole the Christmas Fairy be there too Timothy asked? 'Yes, of course, Thomas said she has to be there, she turns into the Christmas Star so has to be there.'

'I am stupid,' Timothy said I completely forgot that.'

It's so long ago since I have seen the Christmas Spectacle of Carole turning into the Christmas Star. I remember Celine and Catrin telling me a story of how they had a visit from the invisible daughter of Santa and Mamma when she had her accident and could not remember how to change into the Christmas Star but as soon as she put on her special dress everything fell into place, as her friends held her hands and flew up to the heavens with her, her dress seemed to begin to glow and suddenly she became the Christmas Star that had guided the three wise men those many years ago to Jesus who was lying in his crib, in the humble stable with all the animals.

Yes, Thomas said it's the same every year now, instead of Carole flying up towards the heavens herself she now fly's up with her friends holding her hands. Now, how about a nice pot of fairy tea, with some spices, and some of those wonderful, fairy cakes of yours, before I go back to Lapland for the special fairy dust.' So Timothy set to work making the spiced fairy tea and fairy cakes with the special spices he got for Christmas last year. As the two brothers, sat there together, in the warmth of the little red and yellow house, with the little fire burning brightly in the hearth of that November day talking about when they were children in Lapland and helping Santa and Mamma make the toys for Christmas. Lovely wooden toys not like the plastic things they make now laughed Thomas. Yes, the children seem more intent on these electronic things now but they do not get the fresh air like they did when we were younger.

'Well, dear brother Thomas said, I must away now to get back in time to collect the special fairy dust and then bring it back for you.' He sprinkled some fairy dust all over himself and whispered the magic words and then whoosh! He was gone in a flash of blue lightening. Timothy thought to himself, now I must clear up the debris of our tea, but before he knew it the tea cups, saucers plates etc., all disappeared into his kitchen and began to wash themselves in warm water, then dry themselves and put themselves away. Timothy laughed to himself, thinking that brother of mine, give him some fairy dust and he goes mad. 'Well, must go and feed the donkeys their special mix before supper. As he walked towards the little red barn he saw the little donkey walking with his head down as if he was upset. 'Whatever is the matter? Jingles He asked. 'The little donkey said your brother was going to talk to me before he went home as he could not play with me but he's gone and did not speak to me.' Oh! Timothy said he will be back he has just gone to get some special fairy dust from Santa so we can all go to Lapland for Christmas and you will meet lots of fairy folk to talk too, Santa and Mamma and my mother and father amongst them.'

'That is wonderful said the little donkey, he started to jump up and down and turning round and round in his excitement. Timothy left him to his exuberance laughing. The little donkey suddenly stood very still and thought oh! I wish I could fly.' I would be able to go to Lapland then anytime I want. He walked slowly towards the little red barn where his special food mix was waiting for him. 'Timothy he asked 'why can't I fly like Papa and Mama? I do wish I could fly I could go anywhere then.' Timothy answered but you can't or won't be able to fly anywhere anytime he said. 'But, said, the little donkey. 'No, buts about it Timothy said your special powers only available in times of trouble and Christmas. 'I will be able to fly then won't I?' the little donkey Jingles asked. 'Yes, you will Timothy said now come eat your special mix or you won't because this is what helps you with your special powers.'

'I did not know that said the little donkey' neighing. 'Well, now you do' Timothy the little gnome said laughing, and don't you forget it.'

The little donkey was really enjoying his special mix tonight as he munched he dreamed and as he dreamed he saw himself flying across the fields and up to the mountains. Christmas he was going to see Santa and Mamma and all the fairy folk in Lapland. 'What are you daydreaming about my son his mother asked? 'When I can fly' he said neighing. 'Yes, it won't be long his mother said about Christmas time this year you will be able to fly. 'Why Christmas', the little donkey asked? 'Because that was the day Jesus was born and your father was there and so they granted him special powers.'

'Whose they the little donkey asked? 'God the Heavenly Father and all the Angels and Archangels said his mother. It was his special gift from them.'

'That is why I only give birth at Christmas' she said. 'That is our special time.'

'That and in times of trouble or terrible danger to the world.' For soon there will be a terrible fight against evil the angels and archangels will have to use their special powers to defete all the bad in the world, but light will prevail and good will win. Then we will be able to fly and help those in this terrible trouble.' 'Now let's think of nicer things.' 'What about our little trip to Lapland to see Santa and Mamma Claus are you excited she asked? 'Yes, very excited and will the new baby be born at Santa Clauses house? 'Yes, said Saffron his mother.

'I wonder if it will be a baby brother or sister he asked. 'I think it will be a girl this time said his mother I am carrying her different from you.' I can't see her Jingles said. 'His mother laughed at him, I am carrying her in my tummy silly boy she said. 'Oh! Jingles neighed in fun. I thought you meant on your back neigh.....'

'Suddenly, whoosh! A flash of blue lightening and Thomas appeared carrying a big bag of something over his right shoulder.

'Whatever is that Jingles asked 'It's the special fairy dust said Thomas to get you all and the cart to Lapland.'

'Oh! Please let me see Jingles said. 'Thomas put the huge sack down on the ground and opened it carefully the light that came out of that sack shone into Jingles eyes causing him to step back it was so bright. 'Wow, he said it's beautiful all purple, gold green, white, yellow, red, orange, silver, gold so many colours look there is more turquoise, pink, blue. 'Yes, Thomas said Santa and the Little Unicorn of Um' create it from his special cave only they and the fairy folk know about. 'Now I must take it to my brother in order that we may prepare for the journey to Lapland.' He tied the huge sack back up and threw it back over his shoulder and walked towards the little red and yellow wooden house. Opened the door and walked inside calling 'Timothy I am back.' Timothy walked, into the sitting room, and spoke 'hello little brother, nice to see you so soon.'

'Well, now big brother how about something to eat, I could eat a scabby donkey.' 'Well, you will not get a scabby donkey here he said I love them too much. 'How do you feel about a Turkey dinner? He said. I have just finished cooking one.' He laughed 'with all the trimmings of course.'

'Wonderful Thomas said anything I can do to help? 'You could set the table, that's all I had left to do.' 'Alright Thomas said where do you keep everything? 'In that cupboard over there Timothy said pointing to the wonderful black welsh dresser. It had an array of wonderful blue and white plates, cups and saucers on it. 'They are nice Thomas said where did you get those? 'I picked them up on my trip to china it's called a Willow Pattern. Knives, forks, and spoons in the drawer on the left he said. 'Now come sit and eat its ready as he carved the Turkey and handed Thomas a plate full of Turkey, help yourself to vegetables etc., gravy in the boat there to your left. Oh! Wonderful Thomas said as he proceeded to stuff his face with all the wonderful grub as he called it. Thomas had never been very good at table manners he thought too much of his tummy.

Timothy laughed at the thought that came into his head, he saw his little brother with the biggest tummy you have ever seen and he could not stand up. Every time he tried standing up he fell over, giggling with laughter Timothy almost choked himself. 'Whatever is the matter with you' Thomas said. I just had a vision of you bursting your trousers at the seams you are eating that much he said. 'Thomas started giggling then and they both fell about in hysterics.

After dinner they took the dishes to the sink and sprinkled on some fairy dust and left it to do its work. Next time they looked the kitchen was very tidy, everything has put itself away. Now get a good night's sleep said Timothy we have a long way to go tomorrow. Your room is upstairs on the left; bathroom en suite he said all posh just finished it last week. Good Night my brother he said hugging him. Good Night big brother replied Thomas.

Next morning after breakfast they both walked towards the red barn and got out the cart, placed Caesar in the harness and Saffron and Jingles in the cart lying down on hey. They both sat on the seat in front after sprinkling the cart and Caesar with the special fairy dust. Caesar had already had a good helping of hey sprinkled with the special fairy dust to help him on his way. Suddenly, a strange thing happened Caesar sprouted wings, Jingles cried out 'but I thought we could not fly unless in trouble or it was Christmas.'

'Well, in a way we are in trouble because the baby is on its way early, said Timothy. 'Oh! Dear Jingles said how far have we to go, well with the help of the special fairy dust and your father's wings we should be there on a wing and a prayer laughed Thomas. Suddenly, there came a big wind and whoosh they were on their way to Lapland. Two hours later the wind died down and they were gliding gently down to the ground as Caesar folded his wings. They suddenly and just as mysteriously disappeared until they were needed again. Well, Saffron and Jingles you may get out of the cart the stables are just over there. He was just un-harnessing Caesar who then proceeded to follow them to the barn. Timothy and Thomas pushed the cart to the corner of the field, then walked towards Santa and Mamma's house to say hello.' Knocked on the door whereby the little elf appeared and said 'Welcome' do go into the sitting room.' In the sitting room Santa and Mamma were sat enjoying a lovely warm fire, Albert please bring some tea and cakes for our friends.' Then please send one of the gnomes to see to the little donkey and his mother and father please. 'Thank you'. 'Yes, Mamma called Albert as he went to the kitchen. Within a few seconds Albert was back with a tray of goodies and some tea for everyone. 'Shall I pour Mamma said Albert, no thank you Albert I will do it said Mamma you go and have a rest now you have already had a busy day.' So Albert said thank you Mamma and walked into the kitchen and asked for some tea and cakes from the little fairy that Mamma left in charge of the kitchen when she was not there. Will you join me Latita? You need to have a rest too now you have had a rather long day yourself. 'Thank you Albert I think I will.' As they sat drinking and chatting a little gnome came rushing through the door, puffing with all the running. Help! Need some help in the stable Saffron's new baby is having some trouble arriving and I am not strong enough to pull it out myself, he said. 'Ring the emergency bell then said Albert, someone will come then.' So the little gnome went outside and rang the emergency bell which sounded out a loud noise and nearly everyone from the toy workshop appeared shouting what is the emergency? I need some help getting the new baby out of Saffron it's, got a leg stuck and I am not strong enough to pull it out by myself.' 'I can help you said a little voice, my name is Anthony and I am very strong. So they both ran towards the stable with some rope and proceeded to help Saffron by placing the rope onto the stuck leg of the baby whereby they could pull it out. Suddenly like a cork out of a bottle plop! The baby arrived. 'Saffron said Oh! My precious baby, welcome. 'Is that her name Jingles asked? Oh! What a good name thought Saffron, yes, we will call her Precious because that is just what she is.' Suddenly, something wonderful happened Jingles had not noticed but he was so excited that his wings had appeared and he was flying round and round his mother and his sister. My Christmas Wish he neighed, my Christmas Wish has come true I am flying and I have wings. 'Yes everyone laughed you have wings.' It was truly amazing because the wings did not disappear like his fathers had once they had arrived, they did not seem to want to disappear, and they didn't because he had been granted the Christmas Wish he had wished for that his wings when they appeared did not go back until there was trouble or it was Christmas. So Jingles was the first donkey to have permanent wings. That is why they called him the Christmas Donkey and why all donkeys were given bells to wear on their harnesses because his name was Jingles and he loved to wear bells.

Jingle Bells. Get it! Laugh out loud.

THE LITTLE WHITE REINDEER

by Pamela Jones copyright celrinfairies.com 23 Oct 2013

IT WAS A COLD crisp night at the North Pole and a blizzard was heading their way. Santa was helping the elves batten everything moveable down so they would not get blown away. It's a good job they were all dressed in red because that is all they could see. They were all wearing goggles so the snow would not get in their eyes. The hoods on their coats were held on by a scarf tied around their heads. Santa said, right my boys just one more thing check the reindeer and make sure they have plenty of hey and fairy dust to keep them going until the morning by which time I hope the storm will have disappeared. 'Right Santa the elves called back you go in and get a warm drink as soon as we are finished we will be in.' 'Thank you Albert Santa said I think I will do just that.'

As Santa walked towards his beautiful comfortable house with all the lights twinkling and flashing to make sure everyone could find their way to it should they need shelter? He saw Mamma standing in the porch looking out for him; it was getting very late nearly twelve of the clock for everyone to be up.' Mamma heaved a sigh of relief the minute she saw him coming towards the house she waved and went to make him some cocoa. As Santa took off his wet coat and hung it up in the porch to dry he called to Mamma Is it o.k. for you to make a warm drink for the elves tonight dear it's so miserable out there. 'Yes, dear already got the milk on to boil, I had thought of that.' As he sat down by the warm fire and toasted his toes to get them warm he sipped his cocoa and said Mamma what else have you put into the cocoa besides cocoa, he laughed. Oh! Just a little Brandy for medicinal purposes she said. I know you do not normally drink spirits but just this once the blizzard is so cold tonight. I felt it just standing in the porch looking out for you she said.' Santa chuckled to himself Mamma is so kind thinking of keeping me warm, but I must say it's taken the chill out of my bones. Mamma came through to the sitting room and sat in her chair opposite Santa's sipping her cocoa. Albert and the boys are all sat in the kitchen by the range defrosting with a cocoa and Brandy and mince pies she said. Mince Pies but I did not get a mince pie he said.' Would you like one then Papa she said, yes I would said Santa having a little giggle to himself. Watch it dear you're getting tipsy.' 'What on that little amount of Brandy you put in my mug, my magic mug is not even smiling he said so there cannot be that much in it.' Mamma came back with his mince pie on a plate and handed it to him.' Thank you dearest he said giggling.' What are you giggling at she asked? 'You dear he said you have flour all over your chin and forehead, you remind me of a painted Indian.' Oh! You old duffer she said I don't laugh at you when your covered in grease from your toboggan' As she finished her cocoa she said well, dear I am going up now are you staying down here for a while or are you coming up too? I just want to check on the gang he said and then I will be with you my dearest.' Oh! They are alright they'll have eaten all my mince pies by now I will have to make more in the morning I was trying to get ahead as its Christmas next week, but as usual I will be making them all week, chuckling she went up the stairs carrying the lantern she used instead of the candle, she worried about candles but the lantern had glass all around it so even if the candle did move it would not cause a fire. She popped into the bathroom and washed her face and hands and brushed her teeth. Put on her nightie and bed sox and climbed into their big warm comfortable bed with its huge feather duvet, and snuggled down until Santa came and slid into bed next to her. He leant over and kissed her good night, good night sweet princess he said.' Goodnight my prince she replied. Soon they were both fast asleep. As the blizzard howled around the little house, not a sound other than that could be heard.

Next morning Santa got up looked out of the window and gasped, good gracious he said. I can only see half of the barn one side is completely covered in snow. That is going to take some digging out.' Oh! Dear said Mamma you will eat breakfast first dear. 'Of course' Santa replied. Need some energy to dig that out even with the bulldozer.' Mamma came out of the bathroom buttoning up her cardigan and tying on her new apron ready to make his breakfast. 'Porridge, eggs and bacon, toast, do dear she asked.' Oh! Could I have a sausage too he asked in his tiny cajoling voice he used when he wanted something extra.' Mamma laughed of course you can my love, just one. Perhaps, two he said laughing his jolly laugh every time he laughed his tummy looked like a jelly wobbling about on a plate.' Mamma giggled at the thought now what has made you laugh my love? It was your tummy wobbling like a jelly on a plate she said laughing. 'Yes, he said keep meaning to lose some weight but then my suit trousers would fall down and he laughed again.' Breakfast is served my love, she said as Santa sat himself in his favourite chair next to the range and tucked into his huge breakfast. The Porridge was sweet this morning the reindeer milk is so much nicer than cow's milk he said.' Yes Mamma said I got it from 'Hildegard' this morning now she is not feeding her calf she still has plenty of milk.' Holly's calf will be due soon she said it will be interesting to see how her calf turns out.' Well, my dearest I must be off got a lot of work to do shifting all that snow will not be easy even with the big bulldozer, now I must go check that my little gang of elves are ready and then get started.' Santa said. 'Bye' for now see you at lunch, by the way what is for lunch to-day? I am making 'Shepherd's Pie and Sponge pudding and custard Said Mamma. Oh! Boy said Santa one of my favourites. Everything is your favourite Mamma laughed. 'Bye dear have a good day.' She closed the door waving through the glass as he walked away. Then with a sigh she turned and walked to the sink, put in the dishes some fairy dust and water and left it to d its job. The fairy dust washed the dishes, dried them and they flew to where they all lived. Mamma set to and started to make yet more mince pies she made four dozen today, sprinkled them with fairy dust and placed them in the oven. The fairy dust would take the pies out when they were cooked and place them on the table. Leaving Mamma to get on with other things she got out the little hoover one of the gnomes invented and hovered everywhere. Then after putting the hoover back in its place she did the dusting, tidying and polishing until everything was spick and span.

Then after she had put all the things away in the cupboard she decided to make herself a cup of tea. She got the tea into a cup sprinkled on some fairy dust and it did the rest. While she was doing that she got a plate and put one of the mince pies onto it. Picked up her cup and plate and walked to sit in her comfy chair by the fire. The fire never went out because the fairy dust did all the work for that the los, put themselves on the fire and if anything fell off it got the dustpan and brush and tidied up. As Mamma sat by the fire eating her mince pie and drinking her tea she sat thinking what she still had to do. Next week was Christmas and she would be very, very busy. When she had eaten her mince pie and drunk her tea she gathered them up and placed them on the sink ready for the next load of washing up. The kitchen was tidy and so she went upstairs to make the bed and tidy upstairs. She looked into the bathroom and thought Papa you're very untidy as she picked up his pyjamas and hung them on the back of the door along with his dressing gown. She washed and cleaned the bathroom using a combination of fairy dust and water which left everything spick and span up there too. 'Now what shall I do next she thought I know I can wrap the Christmas presents while Santa is not here. So she went into their beautiful bedroom with its poinsettia wallpaper which matched the curtains and bedspread to a tee, Mamma had Christmas all the year round because she asked one of the Gnomes to make her the wallpaper just for that reason. She loved Christmas and because it made her happy. So everything in the house was red, white or green, which were her favourite colours. She was herself dressed in red, today she had on a red dress and cardigan with a white apron with holly printed all over it. Her grey hair had a red poinsettia clipped on one side. Now, she thought where did I put everything, ah! Yes, here we are. She gathered everything up and picked up the wrapping paper, tape, ribbons etc., and went downstairs to the dining room where they had a great big table where she could lay everything out, and started to wrap all Santa's presents. She had made him some new sox and jumper, one of the elves made him a new suit with pockets this time because he had no where to put anything in his other suit and he always had to carry a stupid holdall which he kept leaving behind because he was not used to having it. When she had done all that, she left everything were it was to go prepare dinner. As she walked into the kitchen Santa was coming through the door of the porch he took off his black boots, and hung up his outside jacket and took off his top coat. Helloooo! He called to Mamma who laughed I am already here dear she said laughter in her voice. Now which would you like for dinner cheese, onion and tomatoes on toast or baked beans on toast? With sausages Santa said laughing like a small child. Yes the beans have sausages in them, she had found this delightful snack in the human's supermarket when she had gone to deliver some of her homemade Jam's to them. She always told them to use the money for the sick or injured people. They had a hospital in town which is where the money went too every month on the dot. Mamma was the only one who could produce jam with fruit that had gone out of season, because Mamma could use fairy dust to go anywhere in the world to get it. She made Pineapple Jam, Gooseberry, Strawberry, Blackcurrant, Raspberry you named the fruit she had it. Every time the Manager of the supermarket put it onto the shelves it was gone in a matter of minutes. Mamma laughed I have brought extra to-day I can go and get it if you want it she said. 'Yes please said the manager.' 'It's always the same we put it out and within seconds it's gone.' Well, at least they know it's good. Mamma said as she handed him another box full. Give the money to the hospital as usual Frank. 'Yes, I will do that Mamma and thank you.' Frank said. 'That's alright said Mamma glad to be able to help.' Bye for now then Frank see you again next week. She called as she turned and walked

away. She said Hello to some children and she heard them comment'
that's Mamma Claus you know to their cousins who had come to visit.
'How do you know they asked I saw her standing next to Santa in the
Grotto last year? Mamma laughed and carried on to where the sleigh
was and climbed in. Let's go Prancer Mamma said 'Need to get home
for tea.' Santa will be hungry, and so will all the elves. Yes, Mamma
said Prancer and suddenly they were in the air climbing higher and
higher until they were just a little speck on the horizon. Prancer turned
towards the North Pole and home, he was thinking of his dinner of hey,
carrots and fairy dust. They had to have fairy dust or they could not
fly. Mamma called look Prancer there is the house doesn't it look pretty
with all the light shining and twinkling. 'Yes, Prancer said it does' as
he glided down to where Santa was just outside the barn. 'Hello dearest
he said to Mamma kissing her gently on the cheek. Hello dear she
said giving him a hug. 'Tea won't be long I left it cooking in the oven,
roast chicken tonight only got the potatoes and vegetables to finish off
left them on low and the fairy dust was watching them. 'Whenever
its ready Mamma just ring the bell three times I will hear it. 'We will
have to do dinner in two shifts tonight dear said Mamma, we cannot
fit everyone into this dining room together, we really must get a larger
dining room dear.' Yes, said Santa I have done the plans now all I need
to do is get building tomorrow suit you' he laughed. Wonderful if it's
ready for Christmas we can all eat together this year, won't that be
nice.' Lovely, said Santa whistling as he walked to the house to get his
dinner. Mamma followed him into the house and started to put out
the mashed potatoes, roast potatoes, sausage, bacon peas, sprouts and
carrots. Then handed the plate for Santa to put the chicken on as he
carved it passing it to Albert, who passed it to Alfred, who passed it
to George, who passed it to William, and so it went on down the line
until it reached Simon who was sat next to mamma. So it went on
until everyone had a dinner full to overflowing. I like these new plates
said Santa they keep the meals hot until you have eaten everything, yes
good inventor is Cuthbert, it's amazing what he comes up with, he's
now trying to invent a teapot that keeps the tea warm until you have

finished it laughed Santa. 'Right everyone tuck in. Santa said.' Oh! Albert, would you be so, kind as to pass me the gravy and the stuffing. 'Yes, of course Santa Albert said. 'Thank you.' Albert anyone else want the gravy or the stuffing Santa asked. 'No thank you every one called.

When dinner was over the elves cleared the table and put everything in the kitchen. 'What you need Mamma is a dish washer Fred said. 'I have one dear it's me Mamma said laughing no, the fairy dust does it not me. Fred knew a secret and that was for Christmas this year Mamma was getting a new fangled thing called a dishwasher.' You stacked everything up in the dishwasher shut the door, added fairy dust and salt and it did the rest. Knives, forks, spoons in fact anything you put in there it would wash in very, very hot water.

After dinner, everyone settled down in the sitting room and chatted about all the things they would like for Christmas. Mamma and Santa were keeping an ear out to find out what each elf wanted. Smiling at each other and nodding every time they heard what it was. Mamma said would everyone like a cup of cocoa? 'Of course everyone said yes.' 'No, Brandy in it this time she said. All the elves went awe.........' I do not condone it said Mamma Medicinal only, that means if anyone is sick they may have some if you are not sick you cannot have it.' 'All the elves looked at one another and started squirming around pretending to be sick.' 'Forget it boys she said I know your only playing at being sick so you can get the Brandy.' They all started giggling and laughing along with Mamma and Santa.

Now, my happy little gang of elves off to bed with you lots to do tomorrow, we have more toys to make, reindeer to feed, tidying up the barn etc., etc., Santa said.

Night, Mamma, Santa the elves said in chorus as they went to kiss Mamma good night. They all filed out one after the other until there was just one little elf left, what is it Michael Mamma asked as she bent down to speak to him, Michael kissed her cheek and said I'm not tall enough to reach you up there he said laughing as he skipped out of the door leaving Mamma and Santa laughing. 'Well dear Mamma said I need my bed to she said are you coming up? In a little while Santa said

I want to think about something, what's worrying you dear? Listening to the elves tonight made me think, there are a lot more children out there now I was wondering if we had enough toys, I was sitting here quietly trying to remember who lives at 7 Pilkington Crescent, why isn't that little Marybelle Mamma said. Ah! Yes little Marybelle she wanted a musical bride doll.' I must get straight onto that tomorrow he said. Now, we have remembered he said I can go to bed and not worry. Come my dear lets away to that beautiful bed of ours and cuddle up together. They washed their faces, neck and hands and brushed their teeth, changed into their night wear and each climbed into bed on their side and cuddled up together until they fell fast asleep. Were they stayed until daybreak, as the bright sun shining into the window greeted them with her rays of warmth they both sat up and heard a noise? It was someone calling Santa, Mamma come and look we have the new arrival but something's wrong. Santa threw on his clothes he did not bother washing he was terrified what was going on all the shouting and carrying on. 'Whatever is the matter Santa asked? 'Come see, come and see shouted the little elves, it's a miracle. 'What's a miracle Mamma asked? Look, look there, and as Mamma and Santa looked to where Holly the reindeer had given birth they saw it a baby reindeer of the purest white. 'How can this, be Santa, Mamma asked. 'It's a Devine Message from the Lord Santa Said. 'He told me one year a white reindeer will appear as a signal that a new era has begun, this seems to be it.' The Little White Reindeer stood up and looked around, at all the warm laughing faces looking at him 'Hello' he said my name is 'Silver Star' I am to await the coming of the Christmas Angel. She is not here yet, Silver Star, she is away until next week, what did you want of her for. I am the messenger from God; I am here to fulfil a prophecy. 'What prophecy? They all asked. 'Until the Christmas Angel is here I cannot tell you. Silver Star said. 'Would you like something to eat? I am of my mother she will give me sustenance when I need it.' Silver Star said.

We will all go to the house Santa said. Leave the little fellow in peace with his mother. Silver Star settled down next to his mother to wait for the Christmas Angel's coming. His mother kissed his little head, and whispered I love you to him, I know that 'Mother' he said. 'God told me that you would love me when he spoke to me in your womb.' 'Did he really his mother said smiling?' He spoke more like a prophet than a little reindeer she thought. All through the next few days the little reindeer waited patiently for the Christmas Angel to come home to her parent's house. Nothing troubled him he just sat there patiently waiting, day after day, taking sustenance when he needed it from his mother. Most little reindeers would be running and jumping around like kangaroos', but not 'Silver Star.' He just sat and waited.

Until one day she came to see him, smiling she said I am the Christmas Angel can you see me she asked? Of course I can he said I am like you made of magical energy. So they sat and talked for a while until the Christmas Angels said 'What is the prophecy you wanted to tell me? 'As yet he said I cannot tell you, until 'Christmas Eve' when the moon comes out. I can tell you then and only then. When the Christmas Moon is out she said I will come to you then, the Christmas Angel said. 'That will be fine' he said. Goodbye for now then my friend he said. 'Goodbye' she said waving her tiny hand as she walked away from him.'

Two more days until Christmas Eve Mamma and then he will tell us the prophecy, Carole the Christmas Angel said. 'I wonder what it is' she said. 'Wish I could tell you my love' Mamma said but alas I am not a mind reader. Will you please pass me the flour dear' her mother said. 'Not more mince pies Carole the Christmas Angel' said. 'Afraid so Mamma said the elves and your father keep finding where I have hidden them' Mamma said. 'Well I will tell you what she said when you have finished baking them put them into tins and hide them in my bedroom they won't dare to look in there in case I'm hiding from them, for when I want to I can be more invisible so they cannot see me.' 'Oh! Mamma said I quite forgot you can do that dear, chuckling to herself as the last load of mince pies went into the oven. There are a lot of things I can do Mamma that you do not even know about laughed Carole and I am not going to tell you either she said. In case I want to use them any time. Laughing as she pinched a mince pie from the plate on the table.' Oh! You're as bad as your father Mamma said. I am wondering if leaving them in your room will be any safer' Mamma said laughing at her beautiful daughter. Mamma began to clear up the mess in the kitchen and as she turned she could see another mince pie floating in the air, Carole put that back Mamma said and the crystal laugh of Carole rang out. 'How ever did you know it was me' Carole said. Because Mamma said you're the only one, who is invisible to me, when they want to be.' So Carole put back the mince pie and said sorry Mamma but they are so good you know. 'Yes so everybody says Mamma said. 'I am lucky if I get a look in myself she said, so she picked one up with her cup of tea and sat down by the range and ate it. I do agree with everyone she said they are scrumptious. She had such a job trying not to touch another one that she jumped up and put them in a tin and flew up to Carole's room to leave them there in her wardrobe. 'Yes, Mamma can fly; she has magic powers like Santa.' She finished tidying up the kitchen and started to prepare the vegetables for dinner. I do wish one of the little elves would say they wanted kitchen duties for a change Mamma thought and as soon as she said it who should come knocking asking could she help but little Poppy, such an adorable little creature tiny golden curls all over her head and big blue eyes and a snub nose and cupid lips all in a little round face. 'Yes dear you can help me with the vegetables; perhaps you could peel the potatoes Mamma said.' There is a bowl of water to put them in as you peel them. 'Thank you' said Poppy. She loved helping Mamma in the kitchen especially at Christmas time. 'I have peeled all the potatoes Mamma what next, carrots dear I think, we will need rather a lot as everyone's eating together this year now the new dining rooms almost finished it will be much better. They were just putting the new door on when I was there Poppy said, but they will still have to varnish the floor tomorrow just in time for Christmas Eve.'

'Cannot wait to hear the prophecy said Poppy wonder what it could be? We will have to wait and see said Mamma, only one more day now and we will know.' Right, the next job shelling peas, every time Mamma took a pea pod and opened it, it went pop! Poppy by now was in hysterics, she was scrapping carrots and the carrots were going scrape and peas were going pop so it was scrape pop scrape we are making music in the kitchen Poppy said. Funnily enough Mamma had noticed this why was this happening? She thought this has never happened before. Strange things were happening in and around Santa and Mamma's house, this year. Was it something to do with the prophecy? She wondered.' Now, Poppy I would like you to give the peelings to the pigs please and then you may go and get tidied up for dinner. Thank you for your help you came just in the nick of time I was getting a bit behind as they say.' 'You are most welcome Mamma' Poppy said. Could I help tomorrow too please? I would love that Poppy Mamma said. 'Now scoot.'

Mamma put all the vegetables on to cook, the meat was cooked and standing with a new thing called foil covering it to keep it warm, whilst all the meat juices ran through it before carving. She had already set the tables; everything was ready but the vegetables. So she flew upstairs and changed into her other dress after washing her face etc., she put on a clean apron too and flew back downstairs to check on the vegetables. Nearly ready she said to herself. She took the meat through to the head of the table were Santa sits ready for him to carve. Then rang the bell to tell everyone that dinner was nearly ready so they could wash their hands etc., before coming into the new dining room Mamma was as pleased as punch it looked very festive with all the Christmas garlands around the room. The big Christmas tree in the corner all decorated with lights flashing on and off. Everyone sat down and waited whilst Mamma brought in the vegetables she had made it so they could help themselves tonight. So only the meat plate had to be passed round. 'This looks lovely my dearest Santa said. 'Why thank you, dear Mamma said. She poured the gravy over her dinner and passed it to Santa, who then passed it to Albert who passed it to, oh! You know what I mean, and they all tucked in as if they had never eaten a thing before.

Well, it was Christmas Eve the night of the Prophecy everyone had worked hard all day to get everything ready for Santa's Trip around the world. The sleigh had been checked over everything was in working order, the time clock was checked so that when Santa pressed it time stopped for him to deliver the presents in that place and then started again to get to another. So the time had come for the Prophecy. They were all gathered in the barn around where the little white reindeer stood. Carole the Christmas Fairy was there in her gorgeous silver dress for everyone to see. Her golden hair, gleaming because she had, just washed it the halo, around her head, glinting in the light. All at once a hush came over everyone and the stood in silence waiting.

The Little White Reindeer spoke to Carole the Christmas Fairy this is the message of the Prophecy he said.

PROPHECY

THE BUILDING OF THE WALL OF IT WAS JASPER
THE CITY WAS PURE GOLD, LIKE UNTO CLEAR GLASS'THE
FOUNDATIONS OF THE WALL WERE GARNESHED
WITH ALL MANNER OF PRECIOUS STONES
THE FIRST FOUNDATION WAS JASPER,
THE SECOND WAS SAPPHIRE
THE THIRD WAS CHALCEDONY
THE FOURTH AN EMERALD
THE FIFTH SARDONYX
THE SIXTH SARDIUS
SEVENTH CHRISOLITE
THE EIGHTH BERYL
THE NINETH TOPAZ
THE TENTH CHRYSOPRASUS
THE ELEVENTH JACINTH
THE TWELFTH AMETHYST

AND THE TWELVE GATES WERE TWELVE PEARLS
EVERY SEVENTH GATE WAS ONE PEARL
AND THE STREETS OF THE CITY WAS PURE
GOLD AS IT WERE TRANSPARENT GLASS
I SAW NO TEMPLE THEREIN FOR THE LORD GOD
ALMIGHTY AND THE LAMB ARE THE TEMPLE OF IT

Here is the Prophecy as it was told to me. The Little White Reindeer said. Make of it as you will, I am not the messenger to decipher it for you. I just give the message as it was given to me. Thank you Silver Star' Carole the Christmas Fairy said. 'I will try and decipher it somehow.'

Now, we must get the sleigh ready Santa said, Carole you change your dress and make haste up to the sky its almost time for the Christmas Star to shine' he said. All Carole's angel friends where waiting for her to change and then they could take her to become the Christmas Star. Soon she was ready and Santa and Mamma saw their dear daughter for the last time this year for she would be the Christmas Star until the end of the Christmas Period and then she would come back to them as herself. 'Take care, my pet her Mamma and Papa said. I will, and I love you both Christmas blessings for you all and Carole started ascending into heaven. With her Angel friends holding her hands as when she had her accident and hurt her head. Just before she changed into the Christmas Star she waved, and suddenly her dress disappeared and she became the Christmas Star with all her angel friends around her.

Now boys, let's get on the road Christmas is waiting. Santa and his Elf friend climbed aboard the sleigh and it was Rudolf lead off and up.' Rudolf started running at full speed and as he ran he turned up towards the Christmas Star and away they went waving to Mamma Santa was away across the world delivering his presents to the boys and girls.

The little white Reindeer said, I have done my part for now I must return unto God but I will be back every Christmas Eve until the Prophecy is fulfilled. 'Goodbye everyone he said and vanished as if in a sprinkle of snow.' Goodness cried Mamma Who, what was that. It was a being from the beyond a voice said. 'Who, said that, said Mamma' 'I did said the Little Reindeers Mother before she too disappeared. I thought that was Holly Mamma said. 'No, it was a being who took Holly's place for a time said someone, and then Holly herself turned up saying, have I missed anything. Everyone laughed and went indoors. They got out the Strawberry Tea and had a party to end all parties. That is until Christmas Day when Santa was back after his round the world tour..........